To : ....

From: ....

Thank you from our family to yours.

LUNA'S WINGS

OF WISDOM

MORAL STORIES
COLLECTION

Luna's Wings of Wisdom:
The Leprechaun's Lesson
Moral Stories Collection
Edition: 1

Written by Andre Wahl
Illustrated by Andre Wahl

Designed by Cindi Wahl
Edited by Cindi Wahl

Paperback
ISBN 979-8-89407-006-3
modernbookpress.com

LUNA'S WINGS
OF WISDOM
The Leprechaun's Lesson

MODERN
GLOBAL QUALITY
PUBLISHING
BOOK PRESS

ANDRE
WAHL

CINDI
WAHL

Dedicated to the future leaders of tomorrow, starting with Claire, Adrian, and children across the globe, may the lessons learned from these pages serve as guiding lights, illuminating the path toward a more just and compassionate world.

In a forest glade,

where the trees stand tall,

Lived Luna the owl,

who shared wisdom with all.

Her friend Irene, a bunny so bright,

They frolicked together,

in the soft moonlight.

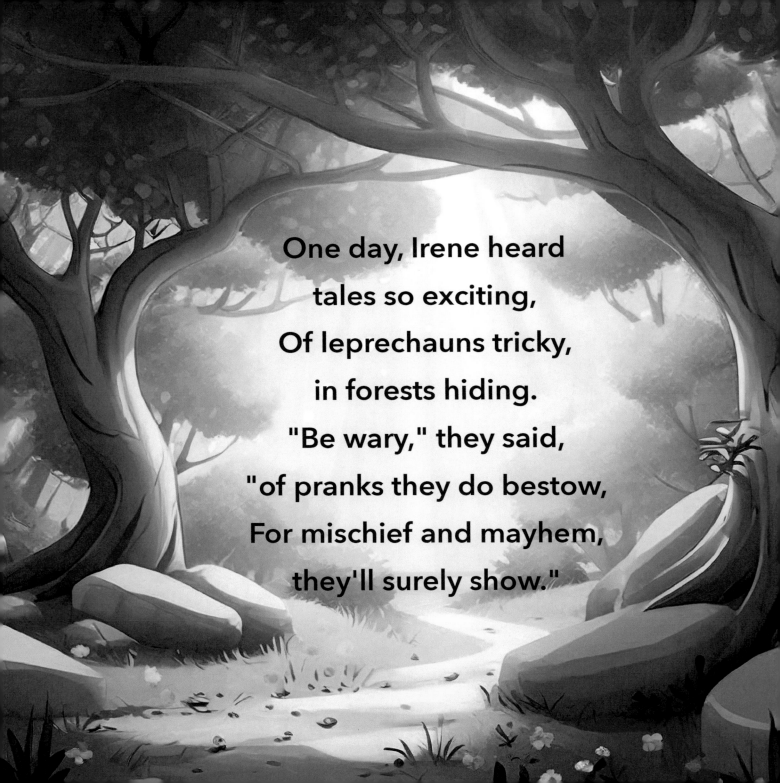

One day, Irene heard
tales so exciting,
Of leprechauns tricky,
in forests hiding.
"Be wary," they said,
"of pranks they do bestow,
For mischief and mayhem,
they'll surely show."

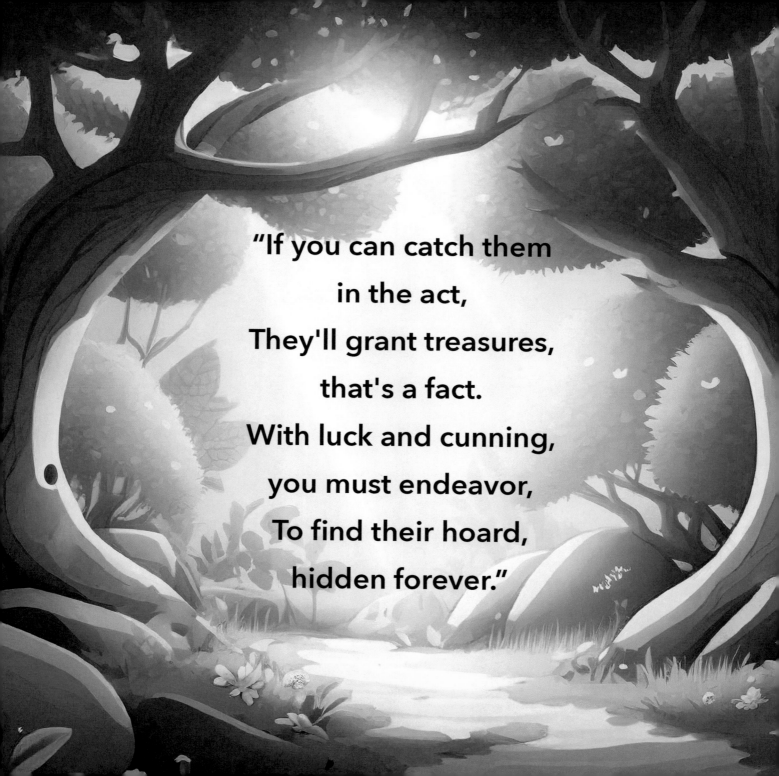

"If you can catch them
in the act,
They'll grant treasures,
that's a fact.
With luck and cunning,
you must endeavor,
To find their hoard,
hidden forever."

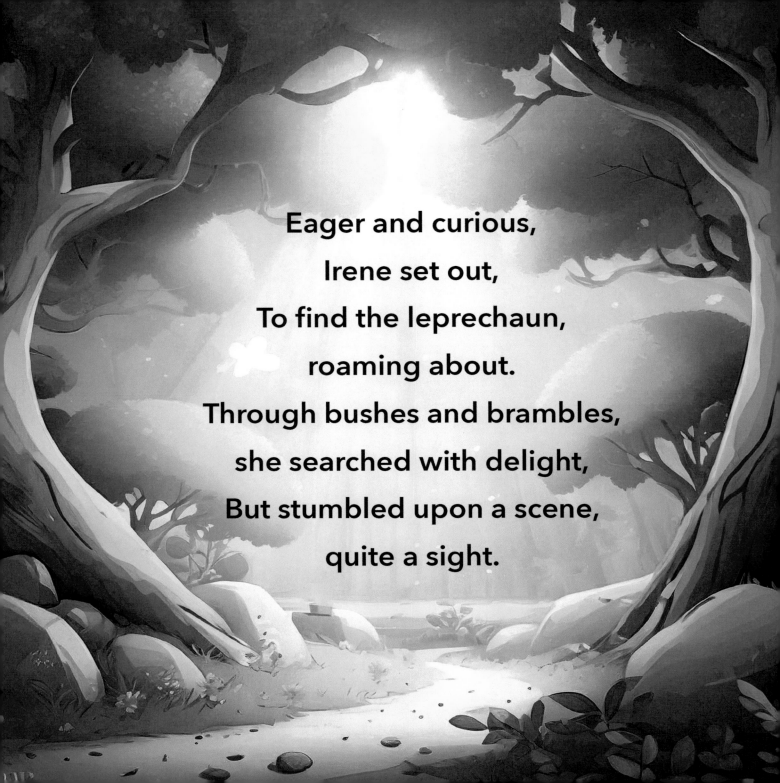

Eager and curious,

Irene set out,

To find the leprechaun,

roaming about.

Through bushes and brambles,

she searched with delight,

But stumbled upon a scene,

quite a sight.

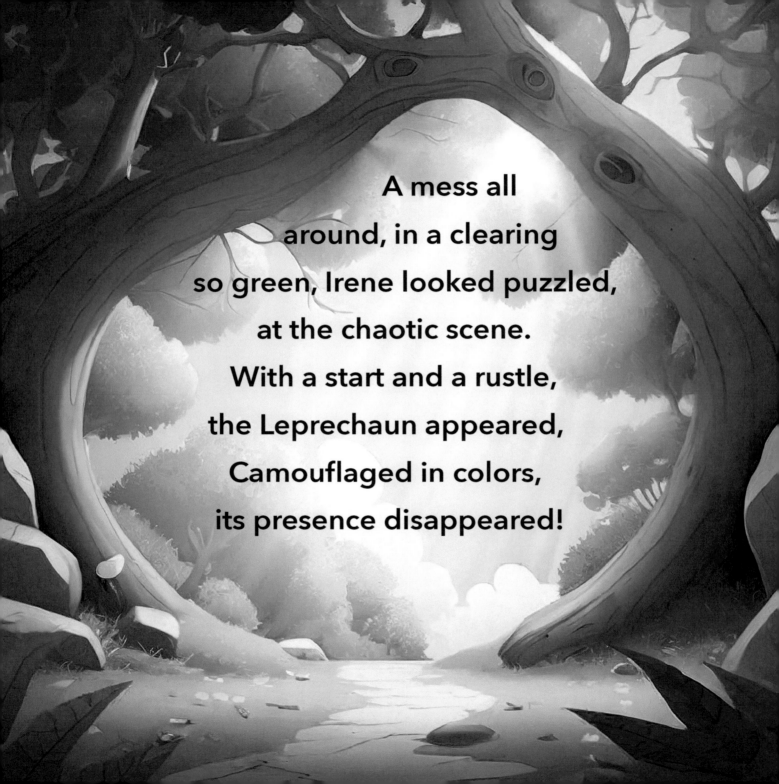

A mess all
around, in a clearing
so green, Irene looked puzzled,
at the chaotic scene.
With a start and a rustle,
the Leprechaun appeared,
Camouflaged in colors,
its presence disappeared!

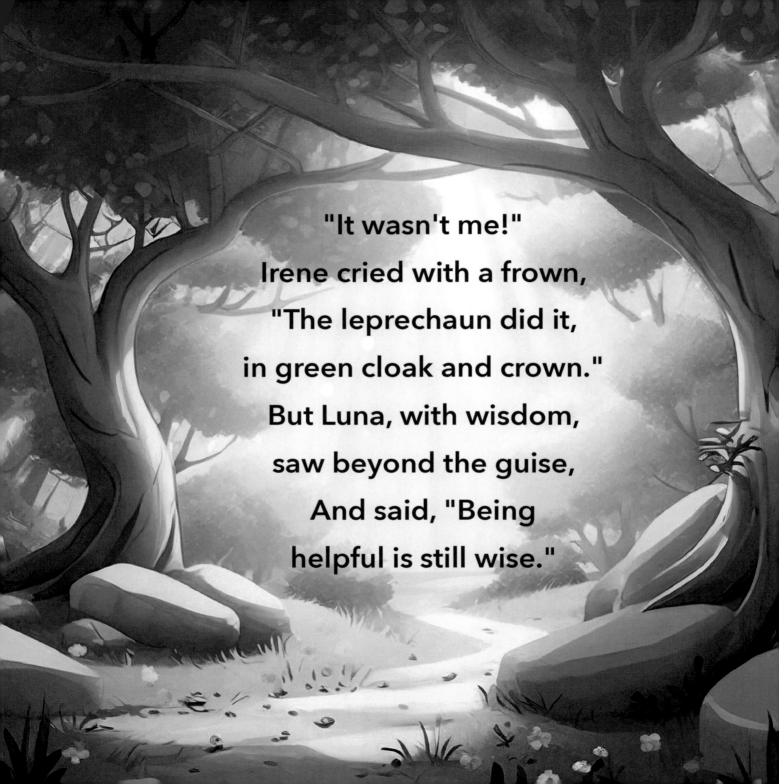

"It wasn't me!"
Irene cried with a frown,
"The leprechaun did it,
in green cloak and crown."
But Luna, with wisdom,
saw beyond the guise,
And said, "Being
helpful is still wise."

Together they tidied,
the mess they found,
The chameleon, grateful,
stayed safe and sound.
As the sun dipped low
and the stars gleamed bright,
The chameleon revealed,
in the soft moonlight.

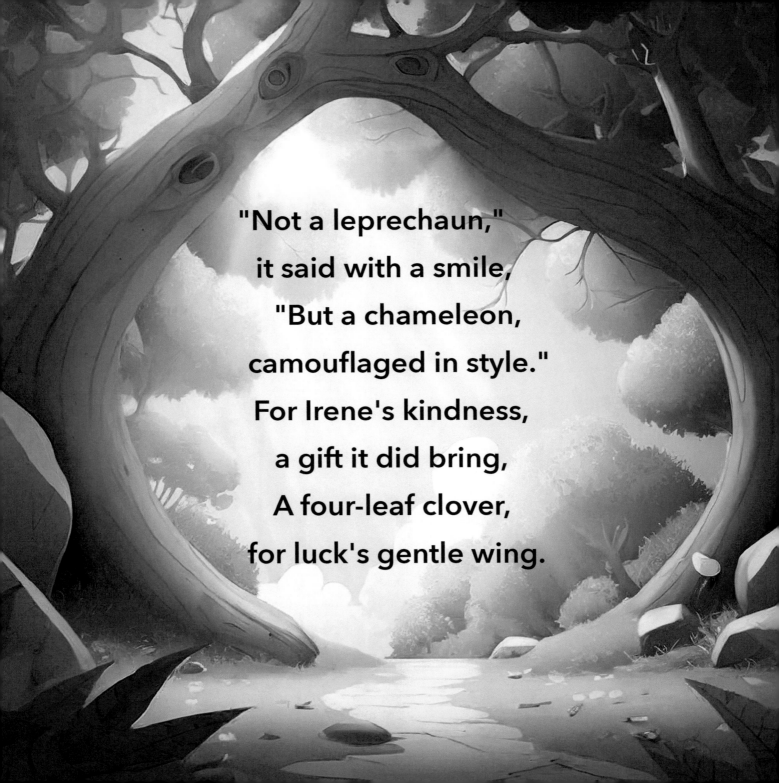

"Not a leprechaun,"
it said with a smile,
"But a chameleon,
camouflaged in style."
For Irene's kindness,
a gift it did bring,
A four-leaf clover,
for luck's gentle wing.

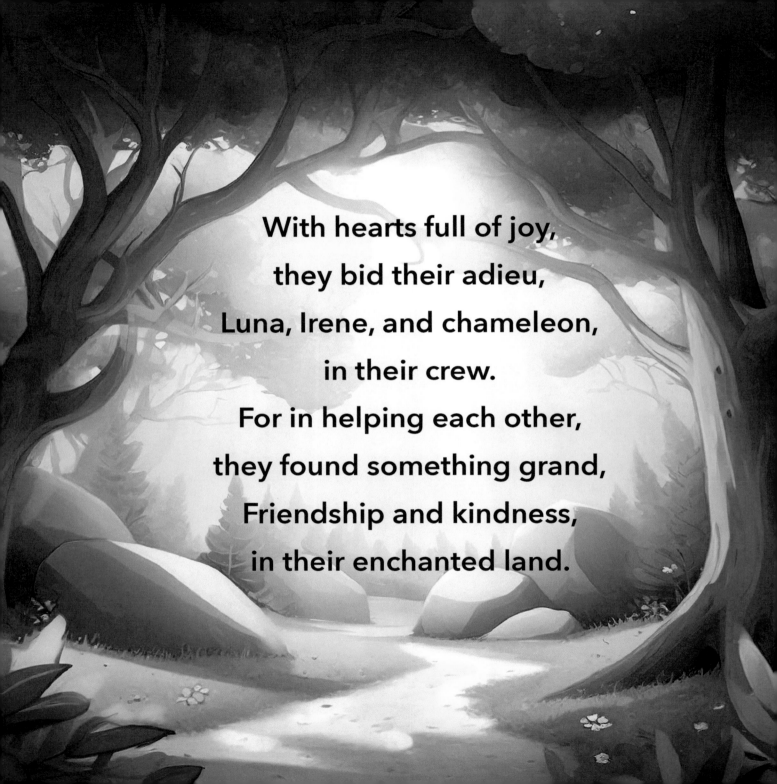

With hearts full of joy,
they bid their adieu,
Luna, Irene, and chameleon,
in their crew.
For in helping each other,
they found something grand,
Friendship and kindness,
in their enchanted land.

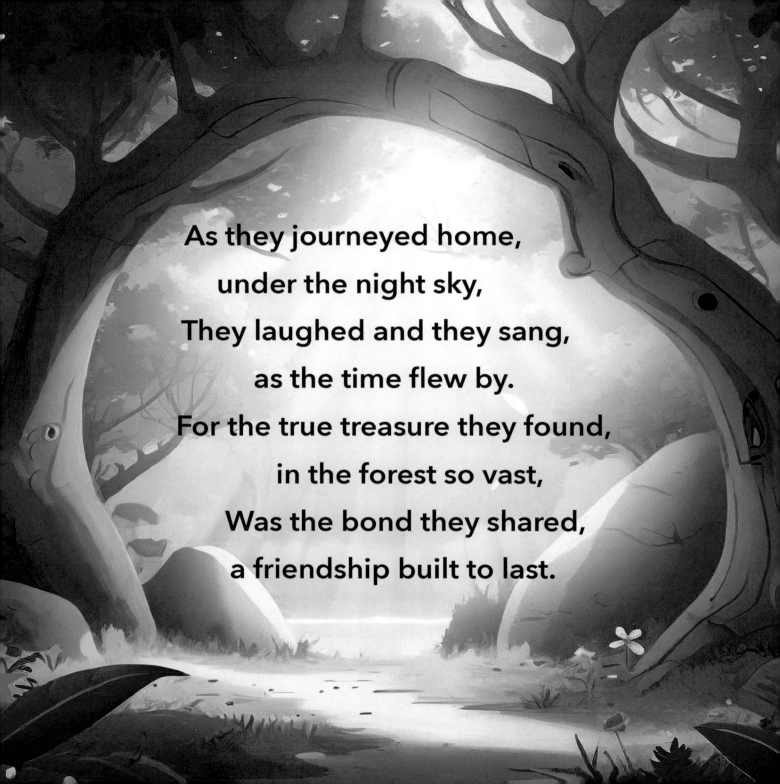

As they journeyed home,
under the night sky,
They laughed and they sang,
as the time flew by.
For the true treasure they found,
in the forest so vast,
Was the bond they shared,
a friendship built to last.

Back in their meadow,
beneath the star's glow,
They recounted their adventure,
with spirits aglow.
And though the chameleon
had vanished from view,
His gift of luck remained,
pure and true.

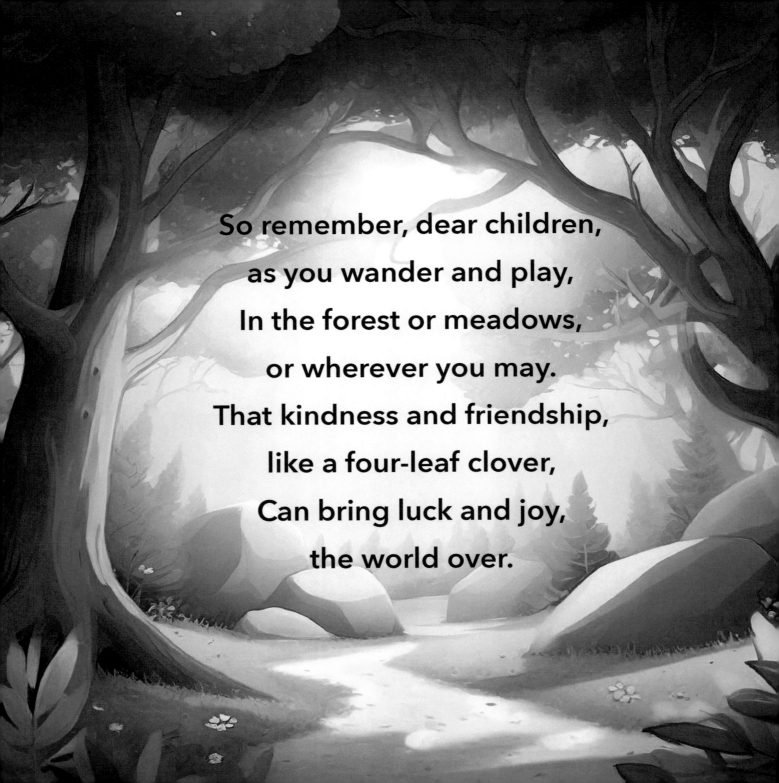

So remember, dear children,

as you wander and play,

In the forest or meadows,

or wherever you may.

That kindness and friendship,

like a four-leaf clover,

Can bring luck and joy,

the world over.

Made in United States
Troutdale, OR
03/10/2025

29638432R00024